MANUELO
THE
PLAYING
MANTIS

Don Freeman

Viking

VIKING

Published by Penguin Group

Penguin Young Readers Group, 345 Hudson Street, New York, New York 10014, U.S.A.

Penguin Books Ltd, 80 Strand, London WC2R 0RL, England

Penguin Books Australia Ltd, 250 Camberwell Road, Camberwell, Victoria 3124, Australia

Penguin Books Canada Ltd, 10 Alcorn Avenue, Toronto, Ontario, Canada M4V 3B2

Penguin Books (N.Z.) Ltd, 182-190 Wairau Road, Auckland 10, New Zealand

First published in 2004 by Viking, a division of Penguin Young Readers Group

1 3 5 7 9 10 8 6 4 2

LIBRARY OF CONGRESS CATALOGING-IN-PUBLICATION DATA

Freeman, Don, 1908–1978.

Manuelo the playing mantis / by Don Freeman.

p. cm.

Summary: A praying mantis who longs to make music gets help from a spider named Debby Webster.

ISBN 0-670-03684-6

[1. Praying mantis—Fiction. 2. Spiders—Fiction. 3. Insects—Fiction. 4. Music—Fiction.] I. Title.

PZ7.F8747Man 2004

[E]—dc22

2003012334

Manufactured in China

Set in Esprit

Book design by Nancy Brennan

MANUELO
THE
PLAYING
MANTIS

ONE WARM SUMMER evening in Cloverdale Meadow, a lonely praying mantis named Manuelo stood still as a stick listening to beautiful music coming over the hill. Manuelo had attended these outdoor concerts many times before, and he knew the shapes and sounds of all the different instruments. His favorite sounds were those of the flute, the trumpet, the harp, and the cello.

Manuelo wished that he, too, could be a musician.

When the concert was over, he climbed down from his perch in the thicket and went home to the pond. Hopefully, Manuelo started rubbing his legs against his wings, the way crickets and grasshoppers and katydids do whenever they sing. But as hard as he rubbed, he heard only silence—and the clicking of a cricket coming nearer and nearer.

"Clickety click!" it chirped. "A mantis can't make music the way *I* can!" And then, just as quickly as it had appeared, it disappeared behind the tall grass.

"There must be something I can do!" Manuelo sighed to himself. Then all at once he thought of an idea. "I know," he said. "I'll make a flute!"

At the water's edge Manuelo found exactly what he needed—a hollow cattail.

In the middle of the pond a frog sat, practicing his singing. He stopped his croaking and watched as Manuelo clipped off one of the tall reeds and nipped several tiny holes along its stem.

But when Manuelo held up his flute and began to blow, not a
sound came through, not even a toot!

"Gerumph! Gerumph!" croaked the frog. "We frogs know how to croak! Now *that* is music! A mantis can't make music the way frogs can!" And with that he jumped into the water.

However, Manuelo hadn't even noticed the frog. His mind was on more important matters, and he set out to find another kind of instrument to play.

Close by, he spied a trumpet vine clinging to a wall. "Just the thing!" he cried. "I'll play a horn!"

After snipping off a trumpet flower he held it up the way any fine trumpet player does, and began to blow. He blew and blew and blew until he grew blue in the face. Once again, not a single sound could he make!

But Manuelo was not going to give up easily. On he went, undaunted. He scanned the ground for something out of which he could fashion a harp. "Ah! At last. Just what I want," he said, picking up a twisty twig that had fallen off a fig tree.

Soon he had bent and fastened the twig into a perfect harp shape. For strings, he found some strands of an old cobweb that had stretched across the lowest branches of the fig tree. . . . Now he was ready to sit down and play his harp.

But when he began to stroke the delicate strands, they broke off one by one—all because of his snippy claws.

No indeed, the harp was not meant to be his instrument!

Poor Manuelo sat there feeling very sad. He loved music so much, and yet he could not make any. At that very moment, three katydids came out into the clearing and began to chant, "Katydid katy, don't you know, a mantis can't make music the way we can!"

Manuelo was discouraged and almost ready to give up trying when he heard something whirring high above his head. "Take heart, my good fellow," said a thin, wispy voice. "I know how you feel. I can't make music either."

Turning his head completely around, Manuelo looked up and saw a spindly spider suspended by a thread from a branch above. "My name is Debby Webster, and I've been watching you all evening," she said as she slid down lower and lower until she hung directly in front of Manuelo's face. "If you will do as I tell you, maybe together we can make a cello. But first of all you must promise not to eat me!"

Manuelo's eyes widened. He had forgotten all about the cello. "Why of course I promise not to eat you." And he meant it. This could be worth a thousand meals!

"All right then," advised the spider. "First you must fetch me an empty walnut shell and a stick with a curlicue on the end."

Without asking any questions, Manuelo went about searching everywhere. In hardly any time at all, he found half a walnut shell and a stick with a curlicue on one end. Tucking them both under his arms, he rushed back to his spindly spider friend.

"Now, my good mantis," said Debby, "if you will fix the stick tightly to the shell I will spin some strong strings for you."

No sooner had Debby whispered this than Manuelo attached the stick to the walnut shell. He watched as the nimble spider spun four strong silken threads from one end of the stick to the other.

"All we need now is a bow," said Debby. "Can you think of something that will do the trick?"

"Yes, yes! I know!" exclaimed Manuelo. "I saw a bluebird's feather that should make a splendid bow." And indeed it did.

At last, Manuelo was ready to play his cello. Taking the bow in
his right hand, he began moving it softly across the silken strings.
And as he bowed back and forth, the most beautiful melody filled the
night air.

Debby swayed to and fro, keeping perfect time to the music, like a pendulum. Gradually from the grassy glade, from behind the fig tree, and from out of the pond, crickets, grasshoppers, katydids, and frogs came creeping forward, making a wide circle around Manuelo.

As they listened, each creature could not resist joining in with the cello's mellow music. Soon everyone was taking part in the concert with clicking, fiddling, wing-singing, and deep-throated croaking. Never was there a more glorious insect symphony!

On and on far into the night, Manuelo played to everyone's delight.

As the first glow of dawn lighted the morning sky, Manuelo rose slowly to his full height and stretched his arms out wide—a sight which served as a warning to the rest of the orchestra to take leave.

Manuelo waited for Debby Webster to slide down inside the hollow nutshell, then he slung the cello over his shoulder and strode across the meadow to his home in the thicket.

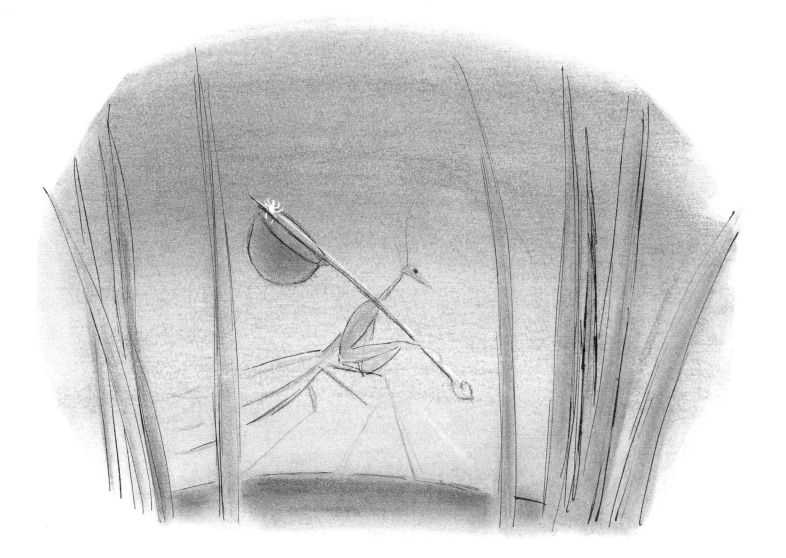

And every summer night thereafter, Manuelo played his cello while Debby swayed back and forth by his side.